TRANSFORMERS ARMADA

OFFICIAL

written by

D1530980

CONTENTS

Reader's Digest Children's Books

Pleasantville, New York • Montréal, Québec • Bath, United Kingdom

The Transformers are a race of intelligent robots that can change their shape, reformatting themselves into vehicles or machines. These shape-changing robots come from the planet Cybertron, which is located in a distant galaxy, far from Earth. For many years, the Transformers lived in peace, aided by a second race of smaller robots, called Mini-cons.

Over the years, the Transformers split into two groups. The first group—called Autobots—believed in the peaceful way of life that had always existed on Cybertron.

A second group—called Decepticons—craved power and domination. They desired control over other worlds, and wanted to eliminate the Autobots. A great war broke out between the Autobots and the Decepticons. Both armies tried to gain control over the Mini-cons, knowing that the Mini-cons increased the power of the Transformers who power-linked with them. The war escalated, and the struggle for control of the Mini-cons almost destroyed Cybertron.

The Mini-cons were loaded on a spaceship and sent into space so no one could ever use their power for war again. The ship crashed on the moon and Earth, where the Mini-cons were eventually activated.

Peace eventually came to Cybertron. But then, when the presence of Mini-cons was discovered on Earth, both the Autobots and the Decepticons traveled there, and resumed their age-old battle.

OPTIMUS PRIME®

FACT FILE

- When Optimus Prime changes into his vehicle mode, he becomes a tractor-trailer truck, possessing even greater strength.

- Optimus Prime's Mini-con partner is Sparkplug, who attaches to the Autobot leader and becomes a state-of-the-art sports car.

- Optimus Prime's Autobot base is located deep in a cave on Earth and is made from a section of the Mini-con ship that crashed there long ago.

PROFILE

Optimus Prime is the leader of the Autobots. He is a powerful force for good and possesses courage, wisdom, and great strength—which he uses in the battle against the Decepticons. Optimus always tries to find a peaceful solution to a conflict, but if a battle is necessary, he becomes a fierce warrior able to overpower nearly any enemy. He is a natural leader, inspiring loyalty among his Autobot comrades. Optimus is the keeper of the Matrix—all the combined knowledge found on Cybertron. The Matrix is an incredibly powerful force.

OPTIMUS PRIME IN VEHICLE FORM

QUOTE:
"FREEDOM IS THE RIGHT OF ALL SENTIENT BEINGS."

▌▌▌ POWER SCALE ▌▌▌	
RANK	10.0
STRENGTH	10.0
INTELLIGENCE	10.0
SPEED	10.0
ENDURANCE	10.0
COURAGE	10.0
FIREBLAST	10.0
SKILL	10.0

SUPER OPTIMUS PRIME®

FACT FILE

- When Optimus Prime is outnumbered during a Decepticon attack, he changes into Super Optimus Prime.

- During a battle at the Autobot fortress, two Decepticons, Cyclonus and Starscream, were no match for Super Optimus Prime.

- When Super Optimus Prime walks, the ground shakes!

- The tractor-trailer truck portion of Super Optimus Prime is incorporated into the base of the robot.

PROFILE

When Optimus Prime converts into his vehicle mode he becomes a powerful tractor-trailer truck. But the Autobot leader has a special power, that only his closest teammates know about. He has the ability to change into a gigantic robot, incorporating his vehicle form into his huge body. This giant robot form is called Super Optimus Prime. As his size grows, so does his power.

SUPER OPTIMUS PRIME IN TRACTOR-TRAILER FORM

QUOTE:
"FREEDOM IS THE RIGHT OF ALL SENTIENT BEINGS."

▌▌▌ POWER SCALE ▌▌▌	
RANK	10.0+
STRENGTH	10.0+
INTELLIGENCE	10.0+
SPEED	10.0+
ENDURANCE	10.0+
COURAGE	10.0+
FIREBLAST	10.0+
SKILL	10.0+

OPTIMUS PRIME® COMBINED

FACT FILE

- Optimus Prime can combine three ways: with his trailer; with Jetfire; and with Overload and Jetfire.

- When Optimus Prime combines with the Transformers robot, Overload, Overload becomes Optimus Prime's shoulder-mounted weapons station!

- Optimus Prime also combines with Jetfire to become an even more powerful robot.

- Optimus Prime's trailer becomes a base that can be used by the Mini-cons.

PROFILE

Optimus Prime can combine with two other Transformers to increase his power. He combines with Jetfire, a robot that changes into a space shuttle. First, Optimus Prime must change into his vehicle form, a tractor-trailer truck. The cab section of his vehicle form remains intact. The space shuttle form of Jetfire rides on top of Overload, connecting to the trailer section of Optimus Prime. Optimus Prime can also combine with Overload, a massive wepons base in both vehicle and robot modes.

OPTIMUS, JETFIRE, & OVERLOAD IN TRAIN FORM

OPTIMUS' TRAILER IN ITS BASE FORM

Sparkplug may be Optimus Prime's main Mini-con partner, but he also relies on Over-Run–a gleaming, silver Mini-con jet who can change into a blaster.

MEGATRON™

FACT FILE

- When Megatron changes into his vehicle mode he becomes a super tank, with incredible firepower.

- Megatron's Mini-con partner is Leader-1, who attaches to the Decepticon leader and becomes a powerful cannon.

- When Megatron tried to wield the Star Saber Sword, he could not control it. (See page 41.)

- Megatron's Decepticon base is located on the moon in a part of the Mini-con space ship that crashed there long ago.

PROFILE

Megatron is the leader of the evil Decepticons. He is the largest, strongest, and most terrifying warrior that the Autobots have ever faced. In his robot form, he can take on an army. In his vehicle form, he has enough explosive power to level an entire battlefield. His goal is to be the ruler of the entire universe, and to destroy planet Earth. To that end, he desires control of all the Mini-cons, which will give him even greater power and abilities.

QUOTE:
"MY POWER IS YOUR DOOM!"

MEGATRON IN VEHICLE FORM

III POWER SCALE III	
RANK	10.0
STRENGTH	10.0
INTELLIGENCE	10.0
SPEED	10.0
ENDURANCE	10.0
COURAGE	10.0
FIREBLAST	10.0
SKILL	10.0

GALVATRON®

FACT FILE

- Galvatron has engaged the Autobots in earth-shaking battles for control of the Mini-cons.

- Galvatron's Mini-con is Clench, a mobile artillery truck.

- Galvatron's huge body contains a prison cell to store the Mini-cons he captures.

- Both Megatron and Galvatron can merge with the Decepticon warship Tidal Wave to gain even more power and weapons! He's a one-robot wrecking crew!

PROFILE

Optimus Prime is not the only one who can change into a powered-up form. Megatron, leader of the evil Decepticons, also changes into a "Super" form. This robot is known as Galvatron. When Megatron changes into Galvatron form, he becomes incredibly powerful. He is even more of a threat to freedom-loving beings everywhere than he was before as Megatron.

GALVATRON COMBINED WITH TIDAL WAVE

III POWER SCALE III	
RANK	10.0+
STRENGTH	10.0+
INTELLIGENCE	10.0+
SPEED	10.0+
ENDURANCE	10.0+
COURAGE	10.0+
FIREBLAST	10.0+
SKILL	10.0+

QUOTE:
"I AM THE POWER OF DESTRUCTION."

GALVATRON IN VEHICLE FORM

RED ALERT™

FACT FILE

- When Red Alert changes into his vehicle mode he becomes an armored rescue vehicle–part ambulance, part tank.

- Red Alert's Mini-con partner is Longarm, who attaches to Red Alert and can grab even the heaviest object.

- During a battle at the South Pole, Red Alert mechanically adapted his Autobot teammates so they could travel in the deep snow.

PROFILE

Red Alert is Optimus Prime's right-hand man. He and the Autobot leader have fought side by side against the Decepticon threat for thousands of years. There is no one that Optimus Prime trusts more than Red Alert. He is a valued doctor, science officer, and mechanic, all rolled into one. His great courage has driven him to risk his own life many times to rescue wounded comrades during battle.

RED ALERT
IN VEHICLE FORM

QUOTE:
"ALL LIFE IS PRECIOUS!"

III POWER SCALE III	
RANK	7.0
STRENGTH	8.0
INTELLIGENCE	10.0
SPEED	7.0
ENDURANCE	8.0
COURAGE	10.0
FIREBLAST	5.0
SKILL	9.0

HOT SHOT™

FACT FILE

- When Hot Shot converts into his vehicle mode he becomes a speedy sports car.

- Hot Shot's Mini-con partner is Jolt, who attaches to Hot Shot as a powerful, turbo-charged helicopter.

- After being adapted to cold-weather environments by Red Alert, Hot Shot was able to drive through deep snow during a battle at the South Pole.

PROFILE

Hot Shot is a young but heroic warrior who is a valuable asset to the Autobot team. He is always impatient for action. Being one of the fastest Autobots, speed is the name of his game. He sometimes rushes into danger without regard for his own safety, and without a well-thought-out plan of action. Hot Shot has taken charge in several battles, used the Star Saber in multiple fights, and has showed great leadership potential. But he sometimes needs the help of an older Autobot like Red Alert.

QUOTE:
"WELL, LET'S GO!"

HOT SHOT
IN VEHICLE FORM

III POWER SCALE III	
RANK	5.0
STRENGTH	6.0
INTELLIGENCE	7.0
SPEED	9.0
ENDURANCE	6.0
COURAGE	8.0
FIREBLAST	4.0
SKILL	5.0

SMOKESCREEN™

FACT FILE

- When Smokescreen changes into his vehicle mode he becomes a huge utility crane.

- Smokescreen's Mini-con partner is Liftor, who attaches to Smokescreen as a front loader/plow combination.

- Smokescreen's entire vehicle has several hidden weapons such as a ramming fist and rocket launchers that combine with his crane arm.

PROFILE

Smokescreen is a loyal friend to Optimus Prime. The two have been through many battles together. He is a large, very strong warrior that moves slowly and deliberately, but packs quite a bit of power into his punches. Smokescreen doesn't waste time in combat with fancy-looking moves. He makes every movement count. His fists and weapons are swinging at full speed— going for an early and decisive blow. His deliberate fighting style works well with Hot Shot's speedy moves.

III POWER SCALE III	
RANK	5.0
STRENGTH	9.0
INTELLIGENCE	7.0
SPEED	6.0
ENDURANCE	8.0
COURAGE	8.0
FIREBLAST	6.0
SKILL	6.0

QUOTE:
"STRIKE HARD, STRIKE STRAIGHT!"

SMOKESCREEN IN VEHICLE FORM

LASERBEAK™

PROFILE

Laserbeak is a protector for Rad, Carlos, and Alexis, the Earth children who witness the Autobots' battle against the Decepticons. He was given to the kids by Optimus Prime. In his spy-bird mode, Laserbeak flies far and wide, recording and transmitting information. In his stun-weapon mode, he can launch fireblasts.

QUOTE:
"I WILL PROTECT YOU."

IIIIIIII POWER SCALE IIIIIIII			
RANK	4.0	ENDURANCE	7.0
STRENGTH	7.0	COURAGE	7.0
INTELLIGENCE	6.0	FIREBLAST	5.0
SPEED	6.0	SKILL	6.0

LASERBEAK IN DIGITAL VIDEO RECORDER FORM

FACT FILE

⦿ Laserbeak transmits information into Alexis' handheld computer, giving her a live video feed so that she can see whatever he is seeing.

⦿ Rad, Carlos, and Alexis once fired Laserbeak in his stun-gun mode at Megatron, blasting the Decepticon leader.

JETFIRE™

PROFILE

Jetfire is an Autobot who is Optimus Prime's executive officer. He is courageous, skilled in battle tactics, and a natural leader. Jetfire understands the individual strengths and weaknesses of each Autobot. He is equally effective on the ground and in the air. In his vehicle form, Jetfire becomes a mighty space shuttle. Jetfire also combines with Optimus Prime.

JETFIRE IN VEHICLE FORM

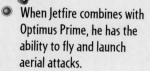

IIIIIIII POWER SCALE IIIIIIII		
RANK	10.0	ENDURANCE 7.0
STRENGTH	8.0	COURAGE 9.0
INTELLIGENCE	10.0	FIREBLAST 9.0
SPEED	7.0	SKILL 10.0

QUOTE:
"YOU CAN FALL ALONE OR YOU CAN FALL TOGETHER!"

FACT FILE

● Jetfire and Optimus Prime are old friends and have fought in many battles side by side. Jetfire has saved Optimus' life many times.

● When Jetfire combines with Optimus Prime, he has the ability to fly and launch aerial attacks.

STARSCREAM™

FACT FILE

- When Starscream changes into his vehicle mode he becomes an incredibly fast jet fighter.

- Starscream's Mini-con partner is Swindle, who converts into a Formula One race car.

- Starscream's arsenal of weapons includes long-range missile-strike capability.

- Starscream was the last of the Decepticons to find his Mini-con.

PROFILE

Starscream is Megatron's second-in-command, and a powerful general in the Decepticon army. Starscream believes that he should be the leader of the Decepticons. He is always looking for ways to weaken Megatron's rule and take the top spot. In battle, he uses speed and maneuverability to launch aerial attacks on the Autobots. He slices through the sky, chasing his enemy, sometimes even endangering fellow Decepticons that get in his way.

QUOTE:
"MY DESTINY IS LEADERSHIP."

STARSCREAM IN VEHICLE FORM

▮▮▮ POWER SCALE ▮▮▮	
RANK	9.0
STRENGTH	6.0
INTELLIGENCE	8.0
SPEED	10.0
ENDURANCE	7.0
COURAGE	8.0
FIREBLAST	7.0
SKILL	8.0

CYCLONUS™

FACT FILE

- When Cyclonus changes into his vehicle mode he becomes an army helicopter.

- Cyclonus' Mini-con partner is Crumplezone, who becomes a tank.

- Cyclonus found his Mini-con partner before Starscream, which made Starscream furious!

- Cyclonus' quickness led to the Decepticons capturing two Mini-cons, right in front of the Autobots' fortress!

PROFILE

Cyclonus is one of Megatron's Decepticon warriors. He is wild, trigger-happy, and always trying to gain favor with Megatron. Cyclonus is so reckless that even his fellow Decepticon teammates are afraid of him. This can be dangerous during a battle, as Cyclonus will suddenly fly off on a chase, leaving his comrades unprotected. Megatron allows Cyclonus his recklessness because he creates confusion during a battle. But sometimes even Megatron himself can't stop Cyclonus once he gets going.

III POWER SCALE III	
RANK	5.0
STRENGTH	8.0
INTELLIGENCE	5.0
SPEED	8.0
ENDURANCE	7.0
COURAGE	8.0
FIREBLAST	7.0
SKILL	5.0

QUOTE:
"OUT OF MY WAY! ATTACK!"

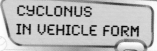

CYCLONUS IN VEHICLE FORM

DEMOLISHOR™

FACT FILE

- When Demolishor changes into his vehicle mode he becomes a missile-launching tank, capable of great destruction.

- Demolishor's Mini-con partner is Blackout, who adds additional firepower to Demolishor's tank form.

- Demolishor has been fighting at Megatron's side longer than any other Decepticon warrior.

- Demolishor has no ambition of his own. This often leads to conflicts with the highly ambitious Starscream.

PROFILE

Demolishor is Megatron's most loyal teammate. He is fiercely devoted to the Decepticon leader, and follows every order Megatron gives him without question or hesitation. Demolishor firmly believes that his leader must be obeyed at any cost—even his own life. Megatron values this unswerving loyalty, but does not hesitate to abandon Demolishor when it suits his own purpose. Demolishor fights with every ounce of his strength and determination. He's a battle-hardened veteran, and is distrustful of the younger Decepticons.

QUOTE:
"AS YOU COMMAND."

DEMOLISHOR IN VEHICLE FORM

III POWER SCALE III	
RANK	7.0
STRENGTH	8.0
INTELLIGENCE	5.0
SPEED	6.0
ENDURANCE	6.0
COURAGE	8.0
FIREBLAST	8.0
SKILL	7.0

RAD, CARLOS, & ALEXIS

PROFILE

Three friends—twelve-year-old bike-riding Rad, ten-year-old skateboard-riding Carlos, and eleven-year-old scooter-riding Alexis—live and go to school at the Cosmo Scope Research Center and Interstellar Observatory in Colorado. Close by is the mountain that contains the Autobot's fortress. While riding through the mountains, they discovered the fortress, and awakened the Mini-cons within. This led to them meeting Optimus Prime, and becoming a part of the Autobots' war against the Decepticons.

FACT FILE

- Rad loves competing in outdoor sports, especially on his BMX bike. He's fearless, but will occasionally rush into danger without a plan.

- Carlos loves skateboarding and hip-hop. He is very courageous, but a bit quick-tempered. Although he's not a great

student, give him a tool and he can fix anything.

- Alexis is by far the best student among the three friends. She always gets great grades, and is a super computer whiz. Her goal is to be president of the United States.

THE MINI-CONS

The Mini-cons are small Transformers robots. When attached to Transformers, they increase the power of all Autobots and Decepticons. When the war between these two sides became too destructive on Cybertron, all the Mini-cons were placed into a spaceship and sent away so that neither side could use their power. The Mini-con ship eventually crashed, first on Earth's moon, then finally on Earth. The Mini-cons themselves scattered all over the moon and Earth. Mini-cons are free agents until they are captured by one side or the other.

FACT FILE

- When Transformers combine with a Mini-con, their power is suddenly increased by a factor of one hundred.

- Mini-cons have been found in caves, on the moon, at the South Pole, inside a volcano, and at the bottom of the ocean.

JOLT™

PROFILE

Jolt is the Mini-con partner of the Autobot, Hot Shot. Jolt takes the form of a helicopter with a turbo-booster. His turbo unit fits onto the front end of his vehicle form. It can also attach itself to the rear of a car, allowing the car to fly. When Jolt combines with Hot Shot, two claw–type arms spring out from Hot Shot's front end, enabling him to slash through enemies or grab hold of objects.

JOLT
IN VEHICLE FORM

QUOTE:	|||||| POWER SCALE ||||||			
"GOTTA HAVE	RANK	5.0	ENDURANCE	7.0
SPEED, GOTTA	STRENGTH	6.0	COURAGE	8.0
HAVE IT NOW!"	INTELLIGENCE	7.0	FIREBLAST	4.0
	SPEED	8.0	SKILL	5.0

FACT FILE

- When Hot Shot combines with his Mini-con Jolt, he can reach incredible speeds.

- When Jolt attaches to Hot Shot he activates a powerful cannon.

- With Jolt's help, Hot Shot was able to distract the Decepticons and lead the Autobots to victory in a critical battle.

LONGARM™

PROFILE

Longarm is the Mini-con partner of the Autobot, Red Alert. In vehicle form, Longarm changes into a crane, which sits atop Red Alert's rescue vehicle. Longarm analyzes and diagnoses technical problems, which Red Alert then fixes. He also helps out during rescue operations, and can activate and launch Red Alert's robotic stun disks.

||||||| POWER SCALE |||||||				QUOTE:
RANK	5.0	ENDURANCE	9.0	"TO
STRENGTH	8.0	COURAGE	10.0	SAVE
INTELLIGENCE	10.0	FIREBLAST	5.0	AND PROTECT
SPEED	6.0	SKILL	9.0	LIFE!"

LONGARM
IN VEHICLE FORM

FACT FILE

◉ Longarm attached to Red Alert and helped him grab a Mini-con out of a lava flow.

◉ When Longarm attaches to Red Alert he activates a powerful weapon that Red Alert shoots from his front bumper.

SPARKPLUG™

PROFILE

Sparkplug is the Mini-con partner of the Autobot leader, Optimus Prime. Sparkplug converts into a superfast sports car and helps Optimus Prime on reconnaissance missions. He also combines with Optimus Prime during battles to increase the Autobot leader's strength.

QUOTE:
"WE MUST ALL LEARN TO LIVE IN PEACE."

IIIIIII	POWER SCALE	IIIIIII	
RANK	5.0	ENDURANCE	9.0
STRENGTH	9.0	COURAGE	10.0
INTELLIGENCE	9.0	FIREBLAST	9.0
SPEED	9.0	SKILL	9.0

FACT FILE

- Sparkplug is in charge of Optimus' trailer when it converts into a base.
- Sparkplug resembles Hot Shot except he is much smaller.

SPARKPLUG IN VEHICLE FORM

LEADER-1™

PROFILE

Leader-1 is the Mini-con partner of the Decepticon leader, Megatron. Leader-1 changes into a piece of self-propelled artillery, capable of inflicting great damage on the Autobots. When Leader-1 combines with Megatron, he becomes an extremely powerful cannon, firing mega-powered blasts.

||||| **POWER SCALE** |||||

				QUOTE:
RANK	5.0	ENDURANCE	9.0	"YOU'RE
STRENGTH	9.0	COURAGE	10.0	GOING
INTELLIGENCE	9.0	FIREBLAST	9.0	DOWN!"
SPEED	9.0	SKILL	9.0	

FACT FILE

- The first time Megatron fired Leader-1, the blast was so powerful that it knocked the Decepticon leader onto his back.

- Additional missiles are available to Megatron when Leader-1 attaches himself to him.

LEADER-1
IN VEHICLE FORM

SWINDLE™

PROFILE

Swindle is the Mini-con partner of the Decepticon, Starscream. Swindle changes into a Formula One race car. When Starscream changes into his jet-fighter mode, Swindle attaches as the tail, adding power to Starscream's attack capability. He also adds stability to Starscream when he is in flight.

SWINDLE
IN VEHICLE FORM

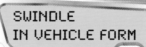

QUOTE:
"YOU WILL
YIELD TO ME!"

▌▌▌▌▌▌▌ POWER SCALE ▌▌▌▌▌▌▌

RANK	5.0	ENDURANCE	8.0
STRENGTH	6.0	COURAGE	8.0
INTELLIGENCE	8.0	FIREBLAST	7.0
SPEED	10.0	SKILL	8.0

FACT FILE

- Starsceam was one of the last Decepticons to get a Mini-con. Finally he found Swindle.

- When Swindle connects to Starscream's jet-fighter body, he activates two very powerful cannons. A cannon is located on each wing.

CRUMPLEZONE™

PROFILE

Crumplezone is the Mini-con partner of the Decepticon, Cyclonus. Crumplezone changes into a powerful tank, with a large cannon in the front. Crumplezone also combines with Cyclonus to become the nose cannon of his helicopter form, increasing the firepower of the Decepticon warrior.

CRUMPLEZONE
IN VEHICLE FORM

▌▌▌▌▌▌ POWER SCALE ▌▌▌▌▌▌			
RANK	5.0	ENDURANCE	8.0
STRENGTH	8.0	COURAGE	8.0
INTELLIGENCE	5.0	FIREBLAST	7.0
SPEED	7.0	SKILL	5.0

QUOTE:
"MOVE OR BE CRUSHED."

FACT FILE

- Crumplezone has helped Cyclonus escape harm in battle many times.

- Crumplezone and Cyclonus pose a doubly dangerous threat—Cyclonus can attack from the sky while Crumplezone launches a land assault.

STREET ACTION MINI-CON TEAM™

SURESHOCK™

GRINDOR™

HIGH WIRE™

FACT FILE

- Both the Autobots and the Decepticons can sense the hidden power of the Street Action Mini-con Team, and so both sides battle to control them.

- Sureshock bonded with Alexis. His vehicle form is a scooter which Alexis now rides.

- Grindor bonded with Carlos. His vehicle form is a skateboard which Carlos now zooms around on.

- High Wire bonded with Rad. His vehicle form is a BMX bike which Rad now rides.

PROFILE

The Street Action Mini-con Team is made up of three Mini-cons: Sureshock, Grindor, and High Wire. These three were the very first Mini-cons to be activated after thousands of years of resting in a dormant state on Earth. Sureshock, Grindor, and High Wire were found by the Earth children, Alexis, Carlos, and Rad, and quickly bonded with the kids. Using their sensors, these three robots have played a key role in helping the Autobots locate other Mini-cons on Earth.

SURESHOCK
IN VEHICLE FORM

GRINDOR
IN VEHICLE FORM

HIGH WIRE
IN VEHICLE FORM

QUOTE:
"SEEK YOUR
TRUE POWER."

III POWER SCALE III	
RANK	5.0
STRENGTH	8.0
INTELLIGENCE	5.0
SPEED	5.0
ENDURANCE	7.0
COURAGE	8.0
FIREBLAST	8.0
SKILL	6.0

AIR DEFENSE MINI-CON TEAM™

SONAR™

RUNWAY™

JETSTORM®

FACT FILE

- Sonar turns into a shuttle craft with rounded lines and two arcing wings in the rear.

- Runway becomes a supersonic transport capable of breaking the sound barrier.

- Jetstorm changes into a jumbo jet capable of traveling at great speeds.

- Jetstorm was found inside a volcano. Sonar was found at the bottom of the sea. Runway was found at the South Pole.

PROFILE

The Air Defense Mini-con Team is made up of three Mini-cons: Jetstorm, Sonar, and Runway. Although their greatest power comes when they combine to form the Star Saber Sword, they each have tremendous power on their own. The three turn into a formidable air-defense machine. In their vehicle forms, they are very effective at flying high-altitude, high-speed missions. The power they bring, both individually and when combined, make the Mini-cons of the Air Defense Team extremely valuable to each side in the ongoing Transformers war.

SONAR
IN VEHICLE FORM

RUNWAY
IN VEHICLE FORM

JETSTORM
IN VEHICLE FORM

QUOTE:
"WE ARE THE
POWER OF THE
SWORD."

▓▓▓ POWER SCALE ▓▓▓	
RANK	5.0
STRENGTH	6.0
INTELLIGENCE	5.0
SPEED	8.0
ENDURANCE	7.0
COURAGE	6.0
FIREBLAST	4.0
SKILL	7.0

PERCEPTOR™

PROFILE

When the three Mini-cons of the Street Action Team—Sureshock, Grindor, and High Wire—combine, they form one larger and more powerful robot called Perceptor. The strength of Perceptor lies in the teamwork of the three Mini-cons who make him up. When Sureshock, Grindor, and High Wire encounter a situation that they are not strong enough to handle individually, they combine to form Perceptor.

QUOTE:
"THE POWER IS WITHIN YOU."

▮▮▮▮▮▮ POWER SCALE ▮▮▮▮▮▮			
RANK	5.0	ENDURANCE	8.0
STRENGTH	8.0	COURAGE	8.0
INTELLIGENCE	5.0	FIREBLAST	8.0
SPEED	5.0	SKILL	6.0

FACT FILE

◉ When the Street Action Mini-con Team combines to become Perceptor, Sureshock becomes the legs, Grindor becomes the body and arms, and High Wire becomes the head.

◉ The first time the Street Action Mini-con Team combined, it was to protect Optimus, Carlos, Rad, and Alexis from Megatron's attack by generating a protective force field.

STAR SABER™

PROFILE

When the Mini-cons of the Air Defense Team—Jetstorm, Sonar, and Runway—combine, they form the Star Saber Sword, a weapon of awesome power. They must be in their vehicle forms in order to combine and form the sword. Sonar forms the handle. Runway forms the lower half of the blade. Jetstorm forms the tip of the blade. It takes great concentration to control the sword. When Megatron tried to use the Star Saber Sword he could not control it. Eventually, the Decepticons learned to harness the Star Saber's power—at that point it became known as...the Dark Saber Sword!

FACT FILE

- Hot Shot was able to control the Star Saber and wound Megatron with its powerful blade.

- Hot Shot was given the Star Saber as a reward for being able to control its power.

- Hot Shot was tricked by Sideways and the Star Saber fell into the hands of the Decepticons.

LAND MILITARY MINI-CON TEAM™

BONECRUSHER

PROFILE

The Land Military Mini-con Team is made up of three Mini-cons: Wreckage, Bonecrusher, and Knock Out. Each of these tough land vehicles carries launchers capable of firing multiple missiles. When launched, the missiles fill the air with streaming trails of explosive destruction. The Autobots fight fiercely to keep these Mini-cons out of the hands of the Decepticons.

BONECRUSHER
IN VEHICLE FORM

WRECKAGE

QUOTE: "LOAD 'EM AND LAUNCH 'EM!"	▍▍▍▍▍▍ POWER SCALE ▍▍▍▍▍▍			
	RANK	5.0	ENDURANCE	7.0
	STRENGTH	8.0	COURAGE	8.0
	INTELLIGENCE	5.0	FIREBLAST	8.0
	SPEED	5.0	SKILL	6.0

WRECKAGE
IN VEHICLE FORM

KNOCK OUT

KNOCK OUT
IN VEHICLE FORM

ADVENTURE MINI-CON TEAM™

RANSACK

PROFILE

The Adventure Mini-con Team is made up of three Mini-cons: Ransack, Iceberg, and Dune Runner. They are a unique team that can combine and fight on any terrain including sand, ice, and mud. Dune Runner has huge gripping tires. Ransack has a grappling hook and towing cable. Iceberg has tank treads capable of traveling on any surface.

RANSACK IN VEHICLE FORM

DUNE RUNNER

▮▮▮▮▮▮▮ POWER SCALE ▮▮▮▮▮▮▮				QUOTE:
RANK	5.0	ENDURANCE	8.0	"NO OBSTACLE
STRENGTH	6.0	COURAGE	6.0	IS TOO GREAT!"
INTELLIGENCE	5.0	FIREBLAST	4.0	
SPEED	6.0	SKILL	7.0	

DUNE RUNNER IN VEHICLE FORM

ICEBERG

ICEBERG IN VEHICLE FORM

RACE MINI-CON TEAM™

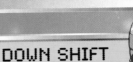
DOWN SHIFT

PROFILE

The Race Mini-con Team is made up of three Mini-cons: Down Shift, Dirt Boss, and Mirage. Individually, these Mini-cons are fast and skilled racing vehicles. But their true might is revealed when they combine. In the heat of battle, they join together to form the shield known as Skyboom. Skyboom is the only known defense against the mighty Star Saber Sword.

DIRT BOSS

MIRAGE

QUOTE:
"COMBINE AND
DEFEND!"

▌▌▌▌▌▌▌ POWER SCALE ▌▌▌▌▌▌▌

RANK	5.0	ENDURANCE	7.0
STRENGTH	6.0	COURAGE	6.0
INTELLIGENCE	6.0	FIREBLAST	4.0
SPEED	10.0	SKILL	7.0

RACE MINI-CON TEAM COMBINED AS SKYBOOM

STREET SPEED MINI-CON TEAM™

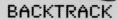

PROFILE

The Street Speed Mini-con Team is made up of three Mini-cons: Backtrack, Oval, and Spiral. They all have one thing in common—the ability to work with precision at record-breaking speeds. These turbo-charged cars are mostly used by the Autobots for reconnaissance missions and quick escapes.

BACKTRACK

BACKTRACK IN VEHICLE FORM

OVAL

OVAL IN VEHICLE FORM

▌▌▌▌▌▌▌ POWER SCALE ▌▌▌▌▌▌▌				QUOTE:
RANK	5.0	ENDURANCE	7.0	"SPEED
STRENGTH	5.0	COURAGE	9.0	OVER
INTELLIGENCE	8.0	FIREBLAST	4.0	STRENGTH!"
SPEED	9.0	SKILL	8.0	

SPIRAL

SPIRAL IN VEHICLE FORM

DESTRUCTION MINI-CON TEAM™

DUALOR

DUALOR
IN VEHICLE FORM

PROFILE

The Destruction Mini-con Team is made up of three Mini-cons: Buzzsaw, Drillbit, and Dualor. Cutting, drilling, and rolling into action, this team creates the ultimate in chaos and destruction wherever it goes. They can also attach to Cyclonus in his helicopter form to maximize their fighting power.

DRILLBIT

DRILLBIT
IN VEHICLE FORM

QUOTE:
"DESTROY AND
CONQUER!"

▮▮▮▮▮▮▮ POWER SCALE ▮▮▮▮▮▮▮			
RANK	5.0	ENDURANCE	7.0
STRENGTH	6.0	COURAGE	6.0
INTELLIGENCE	5.0	FIREBLAST	6.0
SPEED	6.0	SKILL	7.0

BUZZSAW

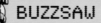

BUZZSAW
IN VEHICLE FORM

SPACE MINI-CON TEAM™

PROFILE

SKY BLAST

The Space Mini-con Team is made up of three Mini-cons: Sky Blast, Payload, and Astroscope. Sky Blast changes into a rocket ship. Payload converts into a rocket transport vehicle. Astroscope turns into a large telescope. The three Mini-cons combine to form the Requiem Blaster, a powerful space weapon.

PAYLOAD

ASTROSCOPE

|||||||| POWER SCALE ||||||||

RANK	5.0	ENDURANCE	7.0
STRENGTH	8.0	COURAGE	8.0
INTELLIGENCE	9.0	FIREBLAST	9.0
SPEED	5.0	SKILL	7.0

QUOTE:
"YOUR DEMISE IS IMMINENT!"

SPACE MINI-CON TEAM
COMBINED AS REQUIEM BLASTER

SIDEWAYS™

PROFILE

Sideways is a ninja-like warrior who changes into a high-speed motorcycle. He is made up of two twin Mini-cons—Crosswise, his good side, and Rook, his evil side. Depending on which Mini-con has more influence at any given moment, he sometimes works with the Autobots and sometimes with the Decepticons. The two Mini-cons also combine to form the motorcycle rider.

SIDEWAYS IN VEHICLE FORM

QUOTE:
"EFFICIENCY THROUGH SELF-SUFFICIENCY."

▌▌▌▌▌▌ POWER SCALE ▌▌▌▌▌▌

STRENGTH	4.0	RANK	6.0
INTELLIGENCE	6.0	COURAGE	8.0
SPEED	6.0	FIREBLAST	6.0
ENDURANCE	5.0	SKILL	8.0

CROSSWISE

ROOK

FACT FILE

- Sideways deceived the Autobots into thinking he was one of them so he could get the Star Saber into the hands of the Decepticon leader Megatron.

- Sideways thinks that Megatron often makes foolish decisions based on anger and not on a well-thought-out plan.